Note to parents, carers and teachers

Read it yourself is a series of modern stories, favourite characters and traditional tales written in a simple way for children who are learning to read. The books can be read independently or as part of a guided reading session.

Each book is carefully structured to include many high-frequency words vital for first reading. The sentences on each page are supported closely by pictures to help with understanding, and to offer lively details to talk about.

The books are graded into four levels that progressively introduce wider vocabulary and longer stories as a reader's ability and confidence grows.

Ideas for use

- Begin by looking through the book and talking about the pictures. Has your child heard this story before?

- Help your child with any words he does not know, either by helping him to sound them out or supplying them yourself.

- Developing readers can be concentrating so hard on the words that they sometimes don't fully grasp the meaning of what they're reading. Answering the puzzle questions on pages 30 and 31 will help with understanding.

For more information and advice on Read it yourself and book banding, visit **www.ladybird.com/readityourself**

Book
Band
6

Level 2 is ideal for children who have received some reading instruction and can read short, simple sentences with help.

Special features:

Frequent repetition of main story words and phrases

Short, simple sentences

Large, clear type

Careful match between story and pictures

Peppa Pig and her family are going on a picnic in the woods. Daddy Pig has the map.

6

7

"We need the picnic, too," says Mummy Pig. But the picnic is still in the car!

8

9

Educational Consultant: Geraldine Taylor
Book Banding Consultant: Kate Ruttle

LADYBIRD BOOKS

UK | USA | Canada | Ireland | Australia
India | New Zealand | South Africa

Ladybird Books is part of the Penguin Random House group of companies
whose addresses can be found at global.penguinrandomhouse.com.
www.penguin.co.uk   www.puffin.co.uk   www.ladybird.co.uk

Penguin
Random House
UK

First published 2013
This edition published 2018
002

This book is based on the TV series Peppa Pig.
Peppa Pig is created by Neville Astley and Mark Baker.
Peppa Pig © Astley Baker Davies Ltd/Entertainment One UK Ltd 2003.
www.peppapig.com

Printed in China

A CIP catalogue record for this book is available from the British Library

ISBN: 978–0–241–20472–6

All correspondence to:
Ladybird Books
Penguin Random House Children's
8 Viaduct Gardens, London SW11 7BW

MIX
Paper from
responsible sources
FSC® C018179

Nature Trail

Written by Lorraine Horsley

Peppa Pig and her
family are going
on a picnic in the
woods. Daddy Pig
has the map.

"We need the picnic, too," says Mummy Pig. But the picnic is still in the car!

In the woods, Peppa sees something on the ground.

"Look down there!" says Peppa. "I can see some footprints on the ground!"

Peppa and her family follow the footprints on the ground.

"A bird made these footprints," says Mummy Pig.

"Look up there in the tree!" says Peppa. "I can see some birds!"

There is a mummy bird and some little birds up in the tree.

Then, Peppa sees
more little footprints
on the ground.

"Look down there!"
says Peppa. "I can see
some ants!"

Peppa and her family are hungry. They need the picnic but it is still in the car.

Daddy Pig looks at the map. "I don't know the way back to the car," he says.

"I know!" says Peppa. "I can see our footprints, too. We can follow our footprints back to the car!"

Then it rains.

The rain takes all the footprints away.

"I know!" says Peppa. "I can see some ducks over there. Ducks love the rain AND they love picnics. We can follow these ducks back to the picnic in our car!"

The hungry family follow the ducks all the way back to the car.

"I love picnics in the woods!" says Peppa.

The birds, the ants and the ducks love the picnic, too!

How much do you remember about Peppa Pig: Nature Trail? Answer these questions and find out!

- Where do Peppa and her family go for a picnic?

- What does Peppa see in the woods?

- Why do the family's footprints go away?

- Who shows Peppa and her family the way back to the car?

Look at the pictures and match them
to the story words.

birds

Mummy Pig

ants

George

Peppa

Daddy Pig

ducks

www.ladybird.com